Dear Parent:
Your child's love of reading starts here!

Every child learns to read in a different way and at his or her own speed. Some go back and forth between reading levels and read favorite books again and again. Others read through each level in order. You can help your young reader improve and become more confident by encouraging his or her own interests and abilities. From books your child reads with you to the first books he or she reads alone, there are I Can Read Books for every stage of reading:

SHARED READING
Basic language, word repetition, and whimsical illustrations, ideal for sharing with your emergent reader

BEGINNING READING
Short sentences, familiar words, and simple concepts for children eager to read on their own

READING WITH HELP
Engaging stories, longer sentences, and language play for developing readers

READING ALONE
Complex plots, challenging vocabulary, and high-interest topics for the independent reader

ADVANCED READING
Short paragraphs, chapters, and exciting themes for the perfect bridge to chapter books

I Can Read Books have introduced children to the joy of reading since 1957. Featuring award-winning authors and illustrators and a fabulous cast of beloved characters, I Can Read Books set the standard for beginning readers.

A lifetime of discovery begins with the magical words "I Can Read!"

Visit www.icanread.com for information
on enriching your child's reading experience.

At the Show

For Laura, who taught me
to ride and show
—C.H.

For Emily
—A.K.

I Can Read Book® is a trademark of HarperCollins Publishers.

Library of Congress catalog card number: 2010938972
ISBN 978-0-06-125542-7 (trade bdg.)—ISBN 978-0-06-125544-1 (pbk.)

11 12 13 14 15 SCP 10 9 8 7 6 5 4 3 2 1   ❖   First Edition

I Can Read!

READING 2 WITH HELP

PONY SCOUTS

At the Show

by Catherine Hapka
pictures by Anne Kennedy

HARPER

An Imprint of HarperCollinsPublishers

It was early morning at the pony farm

where Jill and her parents lived.

Jill had been up for an hour already.

Jill was grooming her favorite pony.

"Hold still, Apples.

I want your mane to look perfect!"

she said with a yawn.

Just then Jill's friends arrived.

"I can't believe I'm up so early

on a Saturday!" Meg said.

"I can't believe Jill is riding

in a real horse show today," Annie said.

Annie and Meg loved ponies

just as much as Jill.

That's why the three of them

called themselves the Pony Scouts.

Meg and Annie helped Jill

groom Apples.

They also helped her pack

for the show.

The girls watched Jill's mom

lead Apples into the horse trailer.

"All aboard for the horse show!"

Meg said happily.

Soon they arrived at the show.

There was a lot to see!

Ponies, kids, and parents were everywhere.

"This is awesome," Meg said.

"Are you nervous?" Annie asked Jill.

"Not really," Jill said.

"Last year Apples and I came in third place

in the eight and under class.

I bet this year we'll win!"

Jill's mom went to sign in

while the girls got Apples ready.

Meg couldn't stop looking

at all the cute ponies.

Meg spotted a glossy bay pony

that was even prettier than the rest.

"Wow, look at that one!" she said.

"He's beautiful," Annie said.

Jill stared at the bay pony.

He looked perfect.

His rider looked perfect, too.

She had fancy riding clothes

and a shiny saddle.

"Uh-oh," Jill whispered.

"That girl looks like a pro!

Maybe Apples and I won't be

winning first place after all."

Jill's friends were surprised.

Usually nothing worried Jill!

"You'll be great!" Meg said.

"Just do your best," Annie added.

"I guess you're right," Jill said.

"Even if we don't win,

Apples and I will still have fun."

Just then Jill's mom came back.

"Jill's class is next!" she said.

There were six ponies in the class.

One was the fancy bay pony.

There was also a tiny pony

with a tiny rider.

First the judge asked the riders

to have their ponies

walk, trot, and canter.

Jill and Apples did great!

Next each rider had to ride over

a row of poles on the ground.

When it was Jill's turn,

she rode Apples toward the poles.

Apples stepped right over each pole,

but he sped up a little at the end.

CLUNK!

His hoof tapped the last one.

Next it was the fancy girl's turn.

She rode ahead proudly.

But when her pony saw the poles,

he stopped short and backed up!

Then he tried to turn around.

The fancy pony was scared.

But his rider kept asking him to go.

Finally the pony went through.

Then came the tiny pair.

The pony stepped over each pole

without touching a single one.

He had to stretch his legs to do it

because he was the shortest.

When the judge gave out the ribbons,

the tiny pair won first place!

Jill and Apples were second.

The fancy girl and her pony won third.

"Good job," the judge told the fancy girl.

"I liked that you didn't give up."

"Both of your ponies were great,"

Jill said to the other riders.

"You guys were great, too,"

the fancy girl said with a smile.

"I hope my pony, Silky,

is as brave as your ponies someday!"

"Don't worry.

He will be," the tiny girl said.

Jill nodded in agreement.

Back home after the show,

the girls groomed Apples

and gave him lots of treats.

Then they hung Jill's ribbon

on the Pony Scouts bulletin board.

"You'll probably come in first place
next time," Meg said.

"I hope so," Jill said.

"Next time, maybe you two
can ride in the show, too!"

PONY POINTERS

groom/grooming: Cleaning

and brushing a horse or pony.

class (at a horse show): A group of

riders competing against one another.

Each separate group makes up one class.

bay: Coloring of a horse or a pony.

Brown with black mane, tail, and legs.

walk, trot, canter: Three ways a horse or

pony can move. Walk is the slowest gait.

Trot is a little faster. Canter is the fastest.